KT-225-118

Contents

To my grandchildren
Michael, Thomas, Robert and Jack

Little Ted Lost

Mary Howard

Illustrated by Amanda Wood

Scripture Union
130 City Road London EC1V 2NJ

© Mary Howard 1995

First published 1995

ISBN 0 86201 971 0

British Library Cataloguing-in-Publication Data.
A catalogue record for this book is available from the British Library.

Printed and bound in Great Britain by Cox and Wyman Ltd, Reading.

Little Ted lost

Simon is four-and-a-bit and lives with his mummy and daddy in a black and white house not far away from the town. He looks very like his Daddy with thick, black hair and lovely gold-rimmed glasses. Last week he was staying with his granny in the country. He had his own little bedroom and he'd brought with him his own Thomas the Tank Engine duvet so that he would feel at home.

At half-past seven it was time for bed. After he'd had his bath, put on his Fireman Sam pyjamas and cleaned his teeth, Simon dashed into his bedroom and jumped on the bed. He looked under his duvet and under his pillow but his teddy wasn't there. 'Where is he, Granny? Where's my Little Ted?'

'I haven't seen him,' she said as she followed him into the room.

Simon hopped off the bed and looked behind the chair and under the bed but he wasn't there.

'When did you last see him?' said Granny as she looked behind the curtains and on top of the chest of drawers.

'I don't remember.' Simon's eyes filled with tears;

he'd never gone to bed before without his little teddy bear.

'Don't worry, I'm sure he'll turn up,' said Granny as she sat on the bed next to him while he said his prayers.

Slowly he crawled under his duvet and started to cry.

'I won't be able to go to sleep without him,' he sniffed.

Granny put her arm around him. 'Well if you find you can't go to sleep, why don't you talk to Jesus about Little Ted? I'm sure he will help.'

'I might,' said Simon pulling the duvet over his head so that Granny wouldn't see his tears.

As she tucked him in bed she asked, 'Now which story are we having tonight?'

Simon wasn't much interested in choosing a story, which was unusual because Granny was good at reading stories – better than Daddy who was always in such a hurry.

'Shall I choose one?' she said.

Simon pulled the duvet from over his head. 'If you like,' he said, but he was more concerned about his Little Ted than listening to a story.

'Once upon a time ...' Granny started to read.

Simon interrupted her. 'Do you think Little Ted might be outside, Granny?'

Granny put down the book. 'Did you have him outside?' she asked.

'I can't remember. I don't think I had him in the garden but I might have taken him to the shops with us. I know I had him in bed last night and I remember taking him down for breakfast.'

'I'll have a look downstairs when I've finished the story and if he's there I'll bring him up to you,' she said and then carried on with the story.

'... and the fox crept into the farmyard and stole one

of the farmer's plumpest chickens,' she read.

'Granny?' Simon interrupted again. 'Do you think someone might have stolen Little Ted?'

'Not if you've left him downstairs,' said Granny.

Simon thought for a moment and then said, 'But some people do steal things, don't they? We learnt at junior church that it's wrong to steal.'

'Why do you think it's wrong to steal?' asked Granny.

Simon thought for a moment and then said, 'Because God says so.'

'Yes,' said Granny. 'He wants us to love each other and give things to each other, not take from each other, which is stealing.'

Granny put her hand on Simon's forehead. 'But I wouldn't worry too much about Little Ted if he isn't downstairs. We'll have a good look for him in the morning. I'm sure he'll turn up,' she said as she kissed him goodnight.

Simon tossed and turned for some time but it was no use he couldn't go to sleep.

'Jesus, I want to talk to you,' he said. 'I can't find Little Ted anywhere. Do you think you could find him for me? He'll be very frightened if he's lost. I can't go to sleep ... 'cos I miss him.' Then he got out of bed and looked behind the door and under the bed once more – but Little Ted wasn't there.

Slowly he climbed back into bed, buried his head in his pillow and cried himself to sleep.

The following morning Granny hadn't found Little Ted so while she made breakfast Simon searched everywhere for him. He looked in the kitchen and in the sitting room; he looked under the chairs and behind the settee; he looked under the cushions and he looked in the toy-box and he even looked in the garden but Little Ted was nowhere to be found.

'Cheer up Simon,' said Granny. 'I'll tell you what we'll do. We'll put a note in the shop window asking anyone who finds Little Ted to return him to this address.' So Granny wrote:

LOST
SMALL BROWN BEAR
IF FOUND PLEASE RETURN TO,
31 HONEYPOT LANE.

Then she read the note to Simon.

'Will that do?' she asked.

'Would you put, "BECAUSE I LOVE HIM VERY MUCH"?' said Simon.

So Granny wrote:

BECAUSE I LOVE HIM VERY MUCH

'You can sign it if you like,' she said. And Simon wrote in his very best writing:

Simon

After breakfast they took the note to the corner shop and Granny paid the shopkeeper twenty pence to display it in the window for one week.

'Now I must call in at the Post Office,' said Granny, 'and post this parcel to Aunty Jean.'

As soon as they walked in the doorway Simon saw him. He was sitting on the counter. 'It's Little Ted!' he cried and ran over to greet him. 'Oh, Little Ted, I thought I'd lost you!'

'He's been sitting here keeping me company since yesterday,' the postmistress told him.

'But we didn't come into the Post Office yesterday,' said Granny.

'No. But old Mrs Jones found him lying on the pavement and thought I might know who he belonged to,' said the postmistress as she looked down at Simon.

'Are you sure he belongs to you?' she said.

'Oh yes. He's my Little Ted.'

'How can you tell? Has he got any special marks or anything that would distinguish him from anyone else's Little Ted?'

Simon thought for a few seconds. 'Not really,' he said and the tears welled in his eyes as he thought that the postmistress might not give Little Ted back to him. And then he remembered something. 'One of his arms is falling off,' he said.

The postmistress picked up Little Ted and looked at his arm. 'You're right. His arm is coming unstitched. He's definitely your Little Ted,' she said and passed him to Simon.

Simon hugged and hugged Little Ted and whispered in his ear, 'I asked Jesus to find you and he showed Mrs Jones where you were. I hope you weren't too lonely without me.'

As they were leaving Granny said, 'Don't you have anything to say to the postmistress?'

Simon ran back to the counter and said, 'Thank you. And please thank Mrs Jones for finding Little Ted.'

'I certainly will,' said the postmistress. 'She'll be pleased to know how happy you are to get him back.'

'And Little Ted's happy too,' said Simon.

'I can see that, but I'll miss him sitting on my counter keeping me company in the Post Office.'

'I'll bring him in to see you whenever I come to stay at Granny's house,' promised Simon.

'I'll look forward to that,' she said.

Simon took hold of Granny's hand and then he said, 'What will happen to my notice now?'

'We'll call at the corner shop and ask the shopkeeper to take it out of the window,' said Granny.

'Do you think she will let me keep it to show

Mummy and Daddy?' asked Simon.

'I'm sure she will,' said Granny. 'Now come along, we'd better go and stitch Little Ted's arm or that will be the next thing to be lost.'

Mummy's birthday

Granny was waiting at the door of the church hall to collect Simon from play-group because Mummy had gone to town to do some shopping. He ran into her arms and she gave him a big hug.

'My goodness I think you've grown!' she laughed.

'Mummy can't pick me up because I'm too heavy.'

'I'm sure she can't. Have you had a good time at play-group?'

'Yes, thank you,' said Simon as he took Granny's hand and skipped along beside her. 'How long are you staying with us?'

'Just for the weekend. I've come over for Mummy's birthday tomorrow.'

'Granny, can I buy Mummy a present for her birthday?'

'Yes, if you like. How much money have you got?'

'I've got fifty pence in my money-box at home. Would that be enough?'

'It depends what you want to buy. We'll call at Mr Gregory's shop and see what he's got for fifty pence. I'll lend you the money, and you can give it back to me when we get home.'

So Simon held Granny's hand tightly as they stood on the pavement and looked to the right and then to the left and then to the right again before crossing the road.

Mr Gregory was a jolly man with lovely pink cheeks and sandy-coloured hair. He was serving a lady in a green hat when they arrived, so Simon walked around the shop to look at the things displayed on the shelves. There were newspapers and magazines, birthday cards, boxes of crayons and colouring books, bars of chocolate and packets of sweets.

'What shall I buy, Granny?' Simon stood on tiptoe to get a better look at the things on the high shelf.

'I think Mummy would like some chocolate or some sweets,' she said.

'How much are these ones?' Simon pointed to the large bars of chocolate.

'They're ninety pence. You haven't got enough money for one of those, darling.'

'What have I got enough money for?' he asked.

'You can have a small bar of chocolate, or fruit pastilles or liquorice allsorts.'

'Oh, they're Mummy's favourites,' said Simon. 'I'll have liquorice allsorts.'

'They're only forty-five pence so you'll have five pence change,' said Granny.

The lady in the green hat left the shop so it was Simon's turn to be served.

'Can I have a packet of liquorice allsorts please Mr Gregory?' he asked politely. 'They're for Mummy's birthday tomorrow.'

'In that case,' said Mr Gregory, 'you'll want them in one of my special bags.' He looked under the counter and brought out a brightly-coloured bag. 'They'll just fit nicely in here,' he said.

Simon handed over the fifty pence and Mr Gregory

gave him five pence change.

'Do you have anything for five pence?' Simon asked.

'I have some little gift cards,' he said rummaging through a box on the counter. 'Ah, here's one that says "Happy Birthday". How will that do?'

Simon looked at the card – it had pink and yellow roses round the edge. 'Yes, I'll have that one. I'll write Mummy's name on it when I get home.'

'Your mummy is very lucky having a little boy to buy her presents and give her cards,' said Mr Gregory. 'You must love her a lot.'

'I do. She loves me a lot as well. Do you wish you had a little boy?' asked Simon.

'Sometimes,' said Mr Gregory.

'I'll ask God to send you one when I say my prayers tonight.'

Mr Gregory smiled. 'I think I'm a bit too old now. And besides I haven't got a wife. Who would look after him while I'm in the shop?'

'Well, when it's your birthday I'll send you a card,' promised Simon.

'And I'll send you one on your birthday,' said Mr Gregory.

Simon was very thoughtful as he walked home with Granny.

'Granny, I wonder why God didn't send Mr Gregory a wife and children to love?'

'God always gives us good things when we ask, maybe God gave Mr Gregory other people instead of a wife and children to love.'

'But we all need someone to love, don't we Granny? I've got Little Ted ...'

'And I've got you,' she said.

When they got home Granny said, 'Would you like

to make a birthday cake for Mummy? We could keep it as a surprise for tomorrow.'

'But where could we hide it?' said Simon.

'Somewhere Mummy doesn't look very often,' suggested Granny.

'I know. On the top shelf of my toy cupboard – Mummy hardly ever looks in there.'

So Granny lit the oven and helped Simon to weigh out the butter, sugar and flour. Very carefully he cracked the eggs into a basin.

Splish, splash, splosh! they went as he stirred them around with a big wooden spoon. It was a lovely sound.

Then he tipped the flour into a sieve and shook the sieve up and down over the basin.

'Look, Granny! Look! It's snowing.'

'It is,' said Granny. 'And you look like a snowman. It's in your hair and on the end of your nose.'

Simon was having a lovely time making Mummy's birthday cake.

'Can I lick the spoon now please?' he said.

'I'd rather you didn't,' said Granny as she put the cake in the oven, 'because the mixture contains raw egg and it might give you tummy ache. I'll tell you what we'll do; when the cake is cooked we'll melt some chocolate and pour it over the top – then you can lick the chocolatey spoon.'

When they'd finished the cake and tidied the kitchen, Granny made a space on the top shelf of Simon's toy cupboard and hid the cake behind his large red tractor. While they were in the bedroom Simon emptied his elephant money-box and gave Granny the fifty pence he owed her.

'What are you doing now?' asked Granny.

'I'm writing Mummy's name on this little card.'

'I didn't know you could write "Mummy".'

'Yes. Daddy showed me how to.'

And so with a little help from Granny, Simon wrote the card and put it in the bag with the liquorice allsorts.

'I'm going to hide the bag under the bed and then it'll be a surprise for Mummy tomorrow. How old will she be, Granny?'

Granny smiled. 'She's as old as her tongue and a little bit older than her teeth,' she said. Simon looked puzzled.

'That's what people used to say when I was a little girl because it was rude to ask older people their age.'

'Will Mummy think I'm rude if I ask her how old she is?'

'Probably not – people don't mind telling their ages these days.'

'So how old are you, Granny?'

'I shall be sixty in November.'

'Is that a lot older than Mummy?'

'Yes. A lot older. I'm twice as old as Mummy.'

Just then Mummy arrived home and Simon ran to meet her.

'How old are you, Mummy?' he asked.

'Who wants to know?' Mummy said as she carried the bags of shopping into the kitchen and plonked them on the table.

'Me. Granny said she is twice as old as you ... and she's sixty.'

'Then if my reckoning is right that makes me thirty,' she said as she ruffled his hair and bent down to kiss him. 'Phew, it's very warm in here. I'll just go and take off my coat and then I think we'll have a cup of tea.'

Granny put the kettle on to boil and took two cups and saucers from the shelf.

'I found out how old Mummy is,' Simon said.

'And?' asked Granny.

'She's thirty. Can we put thirty candles on her birthday cake?'

'I doubt we could fit thirty candles on top of the cake. We could put three – that would be one for every ten years.'

'And I could help Mummy blow them out,' Simon said as he jumped up and down.

The next morning Simon was awake early and he dashed into Mummy and Daddy's bedroom with his present. He jumped on the bed and snuggled down.

'Goodness, who's that with cold feet?' said Daddy as he turned to face Simon. 'Oh, I might have known it was you,' and he tickled Simon under the arms.

Mummy sat up in bed.

'Happy birthday, Mummy! I've brought you a present.'

'Gosh, I'd forgotten it was my birthday,' she said.

'You can't forget your birthday!' said Simon as he handed her the present.

'It's socks,' said Daddy, teasing. 'I can tell it's socks by the shape of the parcel.'

'No, you can't. It's hard and socks aren't hard,' said Simon.

'Oh, it's liquorice allsorts,' said Mummy, as she looked inside the special birthday bag. 'They're my favourites, thank you darling.' And she gave Simon a big hug.

'They're my favourites too,' said Daddy, trying to grab them from Mummy. Simon pushed him away, giggling.

'Well you can't have them – it's not your birthday.'

Simon loved it when Daddy didn't have to go to work. He worked in a big office doing something with computers. Sometimes he worked on Saturday

mornings but not today because it was Mummy's birthday and they were all going out for lunch.

Granny knocked on the bedroom door and came in with a tray of tea and a present for Mummy. It was a lovely scarf that she had knitted and some mittens to match.

Daddy climbed out of bed, knelt on the floor and fumbled around under the bed. Simon joined him.

'What are you looking for?' Simon asked.

'A mouse,' he said as he tickled Simon's toes to make Simon feel like a mouse was tickling his feet. But it wasn't a mouse, it was another present for Mummy. It was the brooch that she'd been admiring in the shop window.

'We've got something else for you, Mummy. Haven't we Granny?' Simon said as he dashed back into his bedroom.

Granny followed him and carefully lifted the cake from behind the big red tractor on the top shelf of his toy cupboard. Simon stuck three blue candles on the top.

'Granny and I made it,' he said as he carried it into Mummy's bedroom.

'It's the nicest cake I've ever seen. I can't think how you managed to make it without my knowing.'

Simon looked at Granny and they exchanged secret smiles!

Mummy's cake

Simon in the kitchen
standing on a chair
making Mummy's birthday cake
flour everywhere.

Sugar in the basin
eggs all slimy yellow
stir and stir and stir it round
what a clever fellow.

Granny come and help me
dollop it in the tin
put it in the oven
then take it out again.

Simon's new baby sister

Simon had a large, black cat called Pushme who would stalk round the garden looking for things to play with as he was very curious. If he didn't find anything he would go and look for Simon.

Today Pushme was especially curious because Simon was packing his blue and yellow duffle-bag full of the useful things he might need on his visit to Granny's house.

Pushme thought it was great fun. He pushed his nose inside the duffle-bag and hid under Simon's colouring book. Then he dragged Little Ted out of the bag.

'Get out, Pushme!' cried Simon. 'You can't come to stay at Granny's house with me, 'cos Marmalade wouldn't like you.'

Marmalade was Granny's large ginger cat.

'You must stay here and look after Daddy while Mummy is in hospital.'

'Miaow,' said Pushme as he pushed against Simon's legs.

'Don't cry. It'll only be for a few days.' Simon bent down and stroked Pushme's head.

'Come along, darling,' called Mummy from the hallway. 'Daddy's putting your case in the car.'

Simon walked slowly into the hall, dragging his duffle-bag behind him.

'Are you all right? You look a bit pale.' Mummy felt his cheek.

Simon didn't answer.

'It's only for a few days and you know how you like staying at Granny's house. And just think when you get back you'll have a baby brother or a baby sister. You've been looking forward to it, haven't you?'

It was true he had been looking forward to it but now he wasn't sure.

'Well, it'll be all right if it's a boy,' he said, scuffing the toe of his shoe on the hall carpet.

'We've talked about this Simon, haven't we? And you know we can't choose.' Mummy bent down and put her arm around him.

'We have to have whatever God sends us.'

'Well, Jeremy got a brother.'

'That was because God wanted Jeremy to have a brother. But if it had been a sister, Jeremy would have loved her just the same. Now have you got everything? Your bricks and your jigsaw puzzles? Oh, and Little Ted; have you got Little Ted?'

Simon nodded his head and Mummy gave him a big hug and kissed him goodbye.

'Be good for Granny,' she said, 'and Daddy will ring you as soon as the baby arrives.'

'Come on, little fellow,' said Daddy as he opened the car door. 'We don't want to get caught in the tea-time traffic.'

Simon jumped into the back of the car and Daddy fastened his seat belt. As they drove away Simon waved to Mummy and shouted, 'Please ask God if I can have a baby brother!'

They arrived at Granny's house at about five o'clock and after Daddy left, Simon sat in the big, warm kitchen and watched as Granny set the table for tea.

'You're very quiet, Simon,' she said. 'It's not like you.'

'I'm missing Mummy,' he said.

'But you've stayed with me lots of times before and it hasn't bothered you.'

'I know, but this time it's different. Mummy is going into hospital ... and I don't know whether I'm going to have a baby brother or a baby sister.'

'Does it matter?' said Granny as she buttered the scones and took a jar of her home-made strawberry jam from the shelf.

'Yes it does. I want a brother like Jeremy, but Mummy said we have to have what God sends.'

'That's true,' said Granny. 'When you were born, God sent us a little boy but it wouldn't have mattered if he'd sent a baby girl – we'd have loved her just the same.'

'Would Mummy and Daddy have loved her as much as they love me?'

'Of course they would. And they won't love you any less when the new baby arrives because we've all got enough love for you and the new baby ... and plenty to spare.'

Simon wasn't sure whether he would have as much love for a baby girl as a baby boy. He knew he loved baby boys because he loved Jeremy's baby brother and he wanted one just the same.

When it was time for bed, Simon sat Little Ted next to him and he and Granny closed their eyes to say their prayers.

'God bless Mummy,
God bless Daddy,
God bless Granny,

and please God when Mummy goes into hospital in the morning to have the baby could I have a little brother?'

It was two o'clock the following afternoon when Daddy telephoned Simon to say that Mummy had a baby girl and they were both fine. Simon didn't know what to say.

'She's lovely, Simon. She looks just like you,' Daddy said. 'She hasn't got a name yet. Would you like to choose one?'

'I don't know any names for girls – only boys.'

'Of course you do. There are a lot of girls at your play-group. They've got names, haven't they? Perhaps one of them has a name you like; and I'm sure Granny knows lots of names. Can I have a word with her now, please?'

Simon handed the phone to Granny and Daddy gave her all the news. When she went back into the sitting room, Simon was on the settee talking to Marmalade.

'I really wanted a baby brother, Marmalade. I don't suppose Mummy can change it now.'

'No, she can't, darling,' said Granny as she sat next to them. 'Come and sit on my knee and we'll talk about it.'

Simon put Marmalade on the floor and climbed on to Granny's knee.

'I asked God for a baby brother,' he said, tears welling in his eyes.

'But we can't always have what we want, dear. It makes us sad at the time but God knows best. He always gives us good gifts. They may not be what we expect at the time but we must trust him. I know you'll love your baby sister when you see her. Now how about choosing a name?'

So Simon told Granny all the girls' names he knew and she wrote them down on a piece of paper and added a few more of her own. He went through them all and finally decided on 'Sally'.

'That's a lovely name,' said Granny. 'Simon and Sally. They sound good together.'

Simon had to agree.

A few days later Daddy came to collect Simon and Granny.

Mummy had asked Granny to go and stay with them for a few days to help with the new baby. When they arrived Mummy was waiting at the door and she scooped Simon into her arms.

'Oh, I have missed you,' she said.

'I've missed you too, Mummy.' Simon hugged her tightly.

'He's been very good,' said Granny. 'And he's chosen a lovely name for his new little sister.'

'Sally! I've chosen Sally,' Simon shouted as he ran into the living room.

Sally lay in a yellow carrycot on the settee, fast asleep. Simon knelt at the side of the cot and gently lifted off the white blanket so that he could see her. She had very tiny feet and as he touched her hand with his finger she curled her tiny fingers around it.

'She likes me!' he smiled excitedly at Mummy.

'Of course she does, she's your baby sister.'

He ran out of the house and into the garden of the house next door.

'Jeremy!' he called. 'Jeremy! I've got a baby sister. Come and see her. She held my hand – she's lovely.'

Jeremy followed Simon into the living room and they both looked into the cot. Jeremy touched Sally's little hand but she didn't move.

'She didn't hold my hand,' said Jeremy.

'That's because she isn't your sister,' said Simon. 'You see she knows that I'm her brother and I love her very much.'

Pushme

PUSHME is my big black cat
his eyes are green and his nose is flat
his whiskers are white
and so are his feet
when he opens his mouth I can see his teeth.

He sits in the garden under the tree
and when I go out there
Pushme pounces at me.

He curls round my legs
and wants me to play
but then sees a leaf and dashes away.

When he is tired
he sits on my knee
and makes funny noises
that sound like a bee.

As soon as he wakes he jumps to the floor
stretches his back and strolls to the door
scratches the wood with the claws on his toes
and where he goes to nobody knows.

Every night at eight!

Marmalade

Granny has a friendly cat
his name is Marmalade
he's big and fat and orange
and his tail's a yellow shade.

He rubs around my ankles
I stroke his furry head
when Granny isn't looking
he climbs up on my bed.

I love him very, very much
and he loves me, I know
'cos when it's time for me to leave
he always miaows, 'Don't go.'

Simon is five

Simon is five today. He is very excited. Mummy and Daddy have given him a farmyard full of animals and he wants to play with it instead of having his breakfast.

'Moo! Moo!' Simon shouted as he moved the cows into the field.

'Come along, Simon, eat your cereal,' said Mummy. 'You don't want to be late on your last morning at play-group, do you?'

'Am I taking a leaving present for Mrs Rogers and Janey?' he asked.

'Yes. I've got them a box of shortbread to have with their coffee and you can take some biscuits for the children to have with their mid-morning milk.'

'What kind are they? Let me see,' said Simon as he looked in the bag on the table.

'They're the ones shaped like animals with coloured icing on.'

'Oh, good. They're my favourites,' he said.

Just then the door-bell rang.

'I'll get it!' Simon shouted, running to the door.

It was the postman. 'I think someone must have a

birthday today. There's a lot of letters addressed to Master Simon Hurst,' he said.

'That's me!' shouted Simon excitedly. 'I'm five and I'm starting school next week.'

'Well, many happy returns of the day,' said the postman.

He handed Simon a large bundle of brightly-coloured envelopes.

Simon dashed into the kitchen to open them. They were all birthday cards. There was one from Mummy and Daddy, one from Granny, one from Aunty Mary, one from Mr Gregory at the corner shop and one from old Mrs Spencer.

'My goodness, what a lot of cards!' gasped Mummy. 'Where shall we stand them?'

'On the windowsill,' said Simon, 'then everyone can see them when they come to my party this afternoon.'

At ten-to-nine Jeremy came to call for Simon to go to play-group. Jeremy lived next door and was Simon's best friend. It was the turn of Jeremy's mum to take them to play-group this morning so they came into the kitchen to wait while Simon put on his coat and collected the biscuits.

'I've got a present for you,' said Jeremy, 'but you can't have it 'til I come to your party this afternoon.'

'What is it?' asked Simon.

'Not telling you. It's a secret isn't it, Mummy?'

'It is at the moment but I don't know whether you'll be able to keep it secret all day,' said Jeremy's mum.

At play-group, Mrs Rogers had made a cake and put five candles on it. The children gathered round and sang 'Happy Birthday' while Simon blew them out. He was sorry to be leaving play-group but excited about starting school.

'I'm having a party this afternoon,' he told Mrs Rogers.

'And I'm going,' said Jeremy. 'I've bought Simon a present but it's a secret 'til this afternoon ... but I might tell him.'

'If you tell him it won't be a secret any more,' said Mrs Rogers. 'And it won't be a surprise for Simon when you give it to him.'

'Does it matter if it isn't a surprise?' asked Jeremy.

'Well, we all like getting surprises, don't we? – especially on our birthday. If I were you, I'd keep it a secret until this afternoon.'

At three o'clock the children arrived at Simon's house for the party. They had each brought a present. Sarah had brought a box of paints and a painting book, Hannah a jigsaw puzzle and James a model aeroplane, but the present Simon liked best was the big, black torch that Jeremy gave him. When he pressed the button on the side, it shone red and everything looked red. But when he pressed it the second time, everything looked blue and when he pressed it the third time everything looked green.

It was great.

Sally, Simon's baby sister, gave him a huge tube of Smarties. Mummy had bought them really, because Sally was too small to buy them herself.

When Simon had opened all his presents, his big, black and white cat, Pushme, slithered underneath the wrapping paper on the floor.

'I think he's looking for a present,' said Daddy.

Simon scooped up the paper and Pushme darted under the table.

'Come along now,' said Daddy. 'It's time for the

games.'

They played Hunt the Slipper, Pin the Tail on the Donkey and Simon's favourite – The Farmer's in his Den.

At four o'clock Mummy shouted, 'It's tea-time!'

'Would you like to thank God for all this lovely food, Simon, as it's your birthday?' she asked.

Simon wasn't sure what to say because Daddy usually said thank you to God at meal times. He looked at the food set out on the table – the sandwiches and jellies and the birthday cake that Granny had made and he said, 'Thank you, God, for my birthday, and Mummy and Granny for my lovely birthday tea, and Daddy for all the fun games we played. Oh, and all my friends for their presents.'

It wasn't quite the same as the prayers Daddy said but Mummy put her arm around him and gave him a big hug.

'You did that beautifully, Simon,' she said. 'Now you can all sit down and help yourselves.'

Simon sat at the head of the table because it was his birthday. Sally had to sit in her high chair but Daddy dragged it up to the table so that she could join the party.

Mummy and Granny poured out fruit juice for everyone and when they'd finished their tea Daddy lit the candles on the cake. It was a round cake, like a clock, with the fingers pointing to five. And it had five candles in the middle. Simon made a wish and then blew all the candles out with one breath.

'What did you wish for?' Sarah asked.

'He can't tell,' said Jeremy. 'It's a secret. If you tell it won't come true.'

Simon decided that he would keep his wish a secret

for ever because it was something he wanted very badly.

After tea Granny disappeared for a few minutes and then came back into the room with a very large parcel.

'Happy birthday, darling. Did you think I'd forgotten your present?'

'No,' said Simon. 'I thought you made my birthday cake.'

'I did. But I've made something else as well. It isn't something you can play with on your own so I thought I'd keep it until all your friends were here.'

Simon was so excited he could hardly open the box – he'd never had such a big present. All the children gathered round him as he carefully lifted out the pieces.

It was a puppet theatre!

There was a stage with curtains and little puppets on strings for the children to work.

'What play are you going to perform for us?' asked Daddy, as he and Mummy and Granny sat on the settee ready to watch the show.

'I don't want to be a performer,' said Simon. 'I want to be the man who draws the curtains.'

'Right, as it's your birthday you can be the man who draws the curtains. We'll call you The Stage Manager, and you'll have to introduce the puppets.'

Simon felt very grand being The Stage Manager.

All the other children took a puppet and dangled it over the top of the theatre so that its feet moved on the stage. They knelt behind the box and disguised their voices so everyone thought it was the puppet who was speaking.

They were having such a lovely time that when their mums and dads came to collect them at seven o'clock they didn't want to go home.

'You can all come and play with my puppet theatre

again, can't they, Granny?' said Simon.

'Of course they can. It would be difficult for you to do all the jobs on your own.'

That night after Simon had his bath and said his prayers, Granny came into his bedroom to read him a story. She found him kneeling on his bed looking out of the window into the starry night.

'Granny, do you think that wishes come true?'

'Sometimes they do,' she said.

'I wished very hard when I blew out my candles ... and when I said my prayers I told God what I'd wished for. Jeremy said you're not supposed to tell anyone but God's different isn't he?'

'You don't need to keep anything a secret from God,' said Granny. 'And it's much better to talk to him than making a wish. But you may have to wait and see what God will give you this time.'

God bless

Hop into bed
you sleepy head.

And snuggle deep.

Pull the clothes
up to your nose.

And go to sleep.

I'll give you a hug
my precious love.

God keep you safe.

Wake up bright
in the morning light.

To his new day.

Simon starts school

It was the first day of the new school term and Simon was awake very early. It was the day he was to start school. His new school uniform was laid out on the chair – grey shorts, blue shirt and navy-blue and yellow striped tie. Downstairs his blazer and cap were hanging in the hall.

Usually he ran into Mummy and Daddy's bedroom when he woke up. But not today. Today he lay quietly, not wanting to get out of bed.

'I wish Jeremy was starting school today,' he said to Little Ted, his favourite teddy bear. 'He can't start until after Christmas because he isn't five yet. I don't think I can take you with me either, even though you are five like me. School isn't like play-group, Little Ted, you will have to stay at home until I get back.'

Slowly his bedroom door opened and in crept Daddy. Simon turned over to face the wall.

'I thought you must still be asleep,' Daddy said. 'You usually come into our room when you wake up.'

Simon didn't reply.

Daddy sat on the bed. 'It's your big day today. You've been looking forward to starting school, haven't you?'

Simon turned towards Daddy and started to cry.

'Hey, this isn't like you,' said Daddy as he put his arms around Simon and gave him a cuddle. 'You're usually a cheery chap first thing in the morning.'

'I won't know anybody at school and I won't know what to do,' cried Simon.

'Don't worry, you'll soon get to know the children in your class. Some of them will be new today and they'll feel exactly like you do.'

'I wish Jeremy was starting with me', said Simon.

'But just think, you'll have made lots of new friends by the time Jeremy starts after Christmas and you'll be able to introduce him to them.' Daddy ruffled Simon's hair.

'I wanted to take Little Ted with me – he's always there just in case I get sad,' said Simon, looking at Little Ted.

'You know who's always there whatever you feel like.'

'Jesus. But I can't see him like Little Ted.'

'No, but that doesn't mean to say he isn't there. He's with us all the time, and ready to help whatever our problem. Remember the time you lost Little Ted and you asked Jesus to help you find him?' asked Daddy.

'Yes,' said Simon as he remembered how old Mrs Jones had found Little Ted and taken him to the Post Office and how he was sitting on the counter waiting for him when he went in with Granny.

'So remember whenever you have a problem always ask Jesus to help.' Daddy gave Simon a big hug and kissed him on the forehead. 'Come along now and get dressed. Mummy has gone downstairs to make the breakfast. I can't wait to see you in your new uniform. I've put a new film in the camera especially to take a photograph of you on your first day at school.'

Simon dressed slowly and then went into his baby sister's bedroom with Little Ted. Sally was lying in her cot kicking her legs. As soon as she saw Simon she started to gurgle.

'I'm starting school today, Sally, so I won't be able to play with you. Do you think you could look after Little Ted for me until I get home? I don't think I'm allowed to take him to school with me – but I've asked Jesus to see if he can sort something out.'

Sally held up her arms and Simon pushed Little Ted through the cot rails.

Simon went into the kitchen and Mummy gave him a big hug and then held him at arm's length.

'Goodness don't you look smart!' she gasped. 'Quite grown up. Are you looking forward to school?'

Simon didn't answer.

'You'll soon make a lot of new friends,' Mummy said as she poured cereal into Simon's bowl.

'But I like my old friends,' he moaned. 'The ones I had at play-group.'

'They were new friends once. It didn't take you very long to get to know them. Come along, eat up your cereal.'

'I'm not hungry,' said Simon.

'Well try and eat a little and I'll put some biscuits in your backpack for you to have with your mid-morning break.'

Daddy came into the kitchen carrying Sally who was carrying Little Ted. Mummy gave her a big kiss and sat her in her high chair.

'What are you doing with Little Ted?' she asked Sally and Sally promptly dropped him on the floor.

'I asked her to look after him for me because I'm not allowed to take him to school,' Simon explained as he picked up Little Ted and handed him back to Sally.

'Who said you weren't allowed to take him to school?' asked Mummy as she poured out two cups of tea.

'Jeremy did.'

'How does Jeremy know? He doesn't go to school.'

'He said he knows.'

'Well, we'll take Little Ted with us and ask the teacher.'

'Can we Mummy?'

'Of course we can. And then if he can't stay with you I can bring him home with me.'

Simon felt much better and began to eat his cereal.

After breakfast Simon stood in the garden and Daddy took his photograph in his new school uniform while Mummy strapped Sally into her car seat.

'Come along, it's time we were off,' called Mummy. 'Don't forget your backpack.'

Simon ran indoors and grabbed it from the hook in the hall. It was a new Thunderbirds backpack that Granny had bought him and inside she had put a pencil, a rubber, a ruler and some coloured crayons. Simon had written his name neatly on a little card and slotted it into the special pocket inside.

When they arrived at school, Mummy lifted Sally out of the car and held Simon's hand as they climbed the steps. Miss Barnes, the teacher, was waiting at the door to greet them. Simon clung tightly to Little Ted as he and Mummy followed her into the classroom.

'Come along,' said Miss Barnes. 'Let me introduce you to Nigel and Victoria. They're starting school today.'

'There's something Simon wants to ask you first, Miss Barnes,' said Mummy.

'Oh, what's that, Simon?'

'Can Little Ted stay at school with me?'

'Of course he can,' said Miss Barnes. 'Lots of children bring their favourite toy with them. They put them over there on top of the cupboard and every day after mid-morning break there's time to play with them together.'

Simon ran over to the cupboard and placed Little Ted next to a doll with long pigtails.

'Now you sit there, Little Ted and watch me in school and then later on I'll come and collect you,' he whispered.

There were lots of different toys on top of the cupboard: a furry rabbit, a wooden train, some building blocks, a black and white panda and a Sooty glove puppet.

Simon ran back to Mummy who was waiting to leave with Sally. She bent down to kiss him and Sally pulled his hair.

'Do you think Jesus made it so that Little Ted could stay at school with me, Mummy?' he whispered.

'I'm sure he did and Jesus will help you to make lots of new friends at school if you ask him.' And with that Simon held Miss Barnes' hand and went over to meet Nigel and Victoria.

Simon makes new friends

Nigel and Victoria were standing near the nature table when Miss Barnes took Simon over to meet them on his first day at school. He had put Little Ted on top of the cupboard with all the other toys.

'This is Simon,' she said, 'and like you, it's his first day at school. The three of you can sit at this table here for a few minutes and get to know one another. The headmistress will introduce you to the other children when we have our assembly.'

Nigel and Victoria didn't speak and Simon didn't know what to say either – he just looked across at Little Ted sitting on top of the cupboard and wished he could go and talk to him. Then he remembered what Mummy had said about Jesus helping him to make new friends.

'Hello, I'm Luke. My Dad's got some glasses like yours. He said I can have some when I grow up. They're great.'

'Well you can't have them if you don't need them,' said Simon.

He was a bit shy of this podgy boy with the red face and hair to match, who had blustered up to the table and plopped down in the chair next to him.

'What's your name? Is it your first day? I started at Easter,' said Luke excitedly.

'I'm Simon and this is Nigel and Victoria. We're all new today.'

Nigel and Victoria didn't speak.

'Do you see that train on top of the cupboard? It's mine,' said Luke.

'That teddy bear is mine; the one sitting next to the doll with the pigtails. I call him Little Ted and take him everywhere with me.'

Luke scraped his chair away from the table.

'Shall we go and have a look?' he said.

Victoria jumped up. *'Don't you touch my doll!'* she screamed, as Luke started to walk towards the cupboard.

'Not now, Luke,' called Miss Barnes. 'Go and sit at your own table please.'

Luke went and sat down.

'What do you call your doll?' whispered Simon to Victoria.

'Belinda. And I don't want anyone to touch her.'

'Those building blocks are mine,' said Nigel. 'After mid-morning break Miss Barnes said we could share our toys so you can both build something with them if you like.'

'And we'll let Little Ted sit and watch us, shall we?'

'Belinda doesn't want to watch,' said Victoria. 'And I don't like building blocks.'

As the clock struck nine Miss Barnes clapped her hands and said, 'Come along everyone, stand in a line. We are going into the hall to have our assembly.'

All the children ran to the centre of the room, shuffled into line and followed Miss Barnes into the hall.

Simon felt very grown-up standing next to Luke.

The headmistress waited until everyone was quiet and then she said, 'We have three new children starting today. This is Simon, and Nigel and Victoria. I want you to show them where everything is in school and after mid-morning break to share your toys with them.'

Luke put up his hand.

'Yes Luke? What is it?' asked the headmistress.

'Please can I show them where everything is?'

'That's very kind of you Luke. Now when you're all standing still we'll sing our assembly song. Today as it's such a lovely day we're going to sing, "Thank you for the world you made".'

Simon was pleased because he knew this song; it was one they often sang at junior church.

Miss Barnes played the piano and everyone sang as loudly as they could.

Afterwards the headmistress said, 'Hands together, eyes closed.' And when they were all ready she said the morning prayer.

'Dear Lord Jesus, please help Simon and Nigel and Victoria to enjoy coming to school. Help us all to make them welcome so that they will very quickly make lots of new friends.'

Then all the children said, 'Amen!'

When assembly was over everyone went back to their classrooms and sat at their tables. Some did painting, some counting and Miss Barnes took some of them for reading.

Soon it was time for their mid-morning break so Simon went with Nigel and Victoria over to the long table at the back of the room. They could choose either milk or orange juice. Simon and Victoria chose milk, Nigel had orange juice.

'Would you like one of my biscuits?' Simon asked as

he went over to his backpack. It was hanging on a peg with his blazer near to the door.

'Can I have one please?' said Luke who suddenly appeared as Simon took out the biscuits. There were four in the packet so they had one each.

After break everyone was excited about sharing each others' toys.

'Come along, Little Ted, we're going over to our table to play with Nigel's building blocks,' said Simon as he lifted Little Ted off the top of the cupboard. Victoria had already collected Belinda and was standing near the table clutching her tightly, not allowing anyone to see her.

'Can I have a look at your doll?' asked Luke.

'No!' snapped Victoria as she put Belinda behind her back.

'You can have a go with my train if you like,' offered Luke.

Victoria put Belinda on her chair and started to push Luke's train around the table.

'Let's make a bridge with the building blocks,' said Nigel, 'and then Victoria can run the train under it.' But as soon as it was finished Victoria crashed the train into it and knocked it down.

'Doesn't your doll get lonely not having any friends?' asked Luke as he peeped at Belinda lying on the chair.

'No, she doesn't.'

'I bet she does. She looks lonely to me,' said Luke.

'Little Ted would be friends with her if you sit her next to him,' said Simon.

'She doesn't like bears,' Victoria said as she ran Luke's train over Little Ted's foot.

Simon picked up Little Ted and Luke grabbed his train and Victoria started to scream with temper.

'Whatever is going on here?' asked Miss Barnes as

she rushed over to the table.

'He won't share his train!' wailed Victoria as she rubbed her eyes with her fist.

'That's not like you, Luke,' said Miss Barnes.

'She ran it over Little Ted's foot,' explained Luke.

'Did you do that?' Miss Barnes put an arm around Victoria's shoulder.

'I don't like bears and Belinda doesn't like them either.'

'What a shame,' said Miss Barnes, 'because I'm sure they like you.'

'Little Ted does. He likes everyone,' said Simon.

'Does he like me?' asked Luke.

'And me?' asked Nigel.

'Yes. He's a very friendly bear.' Simon put Little Ted back on the table.

'He doesn't like Victoria does he, Miss Barnes? Because she ran over his foot with my train.' Luke inspected Little Ted's foot to see that it wasn't damaged.

'He probably does if, as Simon says, he's a very friendly bear. Do you know that Jesus is a friend to everyone, even those who don't love him? How about you all being friendly towards each other?'

'Yes!' shouted Simon and Luke.

Victoria didn't say anything.

'Why don't you put all the toys back on top of the cupboard now because we're going outside to do some gardening,' said Miss Barnes.

'Oh, goody!' cried Luke. 'The other day we found a worm.'

'Yes!' shouted the other children. And then they all sang together:

> *A wiggly, squiggly, wriggly worm.*
> *A squiggly, wriggly, wiggly worm.*

A squiggly, wiggly worm.

When they got outside Luke took Simon, Nigel and Victoria over to the patch of garden where he had planted his seeds earlier in the year.

'These are mine,' he said proudly. 'They're called pansies. We have to take all the weeds out. You can help me if you like.'

Miss Barnes came across to join them.

'They're lovely colours, Luke. The blue ones especially.'

'I like the yellow ones best,' said Victoria who had got over her tantrum.

'I'll give you one if you like,' said Luke, bending down to pick the largest one in the row.

Victoria took it and smelt it.

'That's a beautiful flower, Luke,' said Miss Barnes, 'and very kind of you to give it to Victoria. Doesn't it feel good when people are kind to you, Victoria?'

Victoria nodded.

'I feel good too,' said Luke.

'I expect you do,' said Miss Barnes. 'It's good to be friendly and make friends.'

When they got back into the classroom, Victoria took Belinda off the top of the cupboard and handed her to Simon.

'You can hold her for a little while if you like,' she said to Simon. Then she took Little Ted and stroked his fur.

'Can I hold her next?' asked Luke.

'And then me?' said Nigel who had come to join them.

'You can all hold her in turn,' said Victoria with a smile.

Jesus must be helping Victoria to make friends too, thought Simon.

The jumble sale

During the week before the October half-term there was to be a jumble sale at Simon's school to raise money for the school holiday next year.

'What can I take for the jumble sale tomorrow, Mummy?' Simon asked.

'We'll have to look around and see what we can find. You could sort out some of the toys you've finished with.'

So after lunch Simon went up to his bedroom and took all the toys out of his toy cupboard and spread them out on the floor. Mummy went up later to see how he was getting on. She put Sally, Simon's baby sister, down on the floor and she immediately crawled towards the pile of toys.

'Don't let her touch anything that will hurt her,' said Mummy.

So Simon moved his tractors out of the way because they had sharp pieces sticking out of them. He also moved his pieces of Lego so that Sally wouldn't put them into her mouth and swallow them.

'Shall I take these jigsaw puzzles to the jumble sale?' he asked.

'Yes, if you've finished with them,' said Mummy.

'And some of these books? I've read them all and I got new ones for my birthday.'

While Simon collected the toys together, Mummy looked in his wardrobe and sorted out the clothes that were too small for him.

'I'll look in my wardrobe later,' she said. 'There are probably some things in there that we can take.'

'We'll need a big bag, won't we Mummy, for all these things?'

'We certainly will. I'll take them later in the car.'

Next day was the day of the jumble sale. Simon was up bright and early. It was a Saturday so Daddy was able to go with them. Mummy had been at school the night before helping the other parents and teachers to set out the stalls. There was a stall for toys, a stall for clothes and a stall for cakes that the older children had made in their cookery class.

Mummy and Daddy put Sally in her buggy because they had decided to walk as it was such a nice day. Jeremy and his mummy and daddy and baby brother walked with them. When they arrived at school, Simon and Jeremy ran straight to the toy stall because they had fifty pence each to spend.

As soon as they got there Simon saw it:

A TWO-WHEELER BIKE!

It was blue and had a silver bell. Hanging on the handle bars was a label that said, '£5.50'.

'Daddy!' Simon shouted. 'Look, a two-wheeler bike. Can I have it? Oh, please, please! I've saved enough money.'

'Let's have a good look at it,' said Daddy as he arrived at the stall. 'Mm. It seems in pretty good condition.'

He felt the tyres and tried the brakes. 'Could do with a lick of paint but that's no problem, I could do that.'

'And I could help you,' said Simon jumping up and down.

'How much is it?' asked Daddy.

'Five pounds fifty. Look, it says on the label. And I've got that much. I've got five pounds in my money-box at home and fifty pence you gave me this morning. Can I go home and get the money? Oh, please say yes!' pleaded Simon.

'Is this what you've been asking God for every night when you've said your prayers?' asked Daddy.

'Yes and I've been having little secret talks with Jesus about it too. But I thought perhaps God didn't want me to have it 'cos I've been waiting such a long time.'

'I expect he wanted to make quite sure you were sensible enough to own a two-wheeler bike and remember you're not old enough yet to go on the road with it,' said Daddy.

'I know that and I promise I'll only ride it in the garden or in the park when you're with me.'

'You'll need a helmet too – you can't ride it without a helmet,' said Daddy.

'I haven't got enough money for a helmet yet but I promise I'll save up for one if you'll let me have the bike.'

'I'll tell you what I'll do,' said Daddy. 'I'll let you earn the money for a helmet by doing jobs to help Mummy and me. But so that you won't have to wait to ride your bike, I'll lend you the money and you can pay me back every time you get paid for a job. How does that sound?'

Simon was so excited, he couldn't believe that he was going to get what he'd asked God for.

'We'll have a little book, Daddy, and every time I

earn money for doing a job we'll write it down and then I'll know when I've finished paying for my helmet.'

'Good idea,' said Daddy.

'Can I go and empty my money-box now please?'

But Simon was afraid the bike might be sold before he got back with his money so he decided to ask the lady on the stall to save it for him.

'Why don't you leave your fifty pence as a deposit and then she'll know that you definitely want to buy it,' suggested Daddy.

So this is what he did.

When the jumble sale was over they all walked home. Simon pushed his bike along the pavement and Jeremy walked beside him.

'Was that what you wished for on your birthday?' asked Jeremy.

'Yes,' said Simon. 'But Granny said that I should ask God. He knows best what we need.'

When they got home Simon ran to the telephone.

'Who are you ringing?' asked Mummy as she lifted Sally out of her buggy.

'Granny,' said Simon, 'to tell her I've got my bike.'

Simon could hear the telephone ringing in Granny's house. As soon as she picked up the receiver Simon shouted down the telephone, 'Granny, Granny, I've got what I asked God for!'

'Oh, darling, I'm so pleased. What is it?'

'A two-wheeler bike – and I'm going to help Daddy paint it. I got it from the jumble sale at school. I spent my savings on it. Daddy's going to lend me the money for a helmet and I'm going to pay him back. I'm going to do jobs to earn money and I'm going to have a book and write down how much I earn.'

'What a good idea,' said Granny.

'God must have wanted me to have a two-wheeler bike, mustn't he Granny? Otherwise it wouldn't have been for sale, would it? and I wouldn't have had enough money to buy it.'

'I'm sure you're right,' she said.

Simon put down the receiver and dashed into the bathroom where Sally was having her bath. He knelt down with Mummy at the side of the bath.

'I've got a two-wheeler bike, Sally,' he said. 'And when you're big, like me, I'll let you ride it.'

Sally gurgled and splashed water on Simon and Mummy.

That night Simon sat on his bed and said, 'Thank you God for my lovely blue bike. It's great. And thank you for Sally. I love her very much.'

Sally

Sally's in the bath pink and podgy
wet and soapy like a slippery fish.

Grabbing at the water.

Gurgling and laughing,

Kicking and splashing.

Bubbles everywhere.

On her nose
and in her hair.

In her eyes

and then she cries.

The Nativity play

It was Simon's first Christmas at school and he was getting quite excited. The children had been making Christmas decorations and telling one another what presents they hoped to get on Christmas morning.

'What are you getting?' Simon asked Luke, his best friend.

'I'm not sure. I really want a Scalextric, but Mummy said they're very expensive so I might have to share one with Ben.'

Ben was Luke's older brother.

'I think I might ask for a train set,' said Simon.

'I'm having a doll's buggy for Belinda,' said Victoria. 'She has a pram but she's getting too big for it now.'

Suddenly Miss Barnes, the teacher, clapped her hands and said, 'Come along now everyone, settle down. I have something very special to discuss with you. Come and sit on the floor around me so that you can all hear.'

Miss Barnes sat on her chair and the children shuffled and pushed so that they could sit as near to her as possible.

When they were all quiet she said, 'Now then, who

knows what we are going to be celebrating very soon?'

'I know, I know!' said Luke excitedly. 'Christmas.'

'Right,' said Miss Barnes. 'And what's so special about Christmas?'

'We all get presents,' said Victoria.

'Why?' Miss Barnes waited while they thought about this question.

'Is it because it's a special day?' asked Luke.

'It is a special day – it's a very special birthday. It's the birthday of someone who was born hundreds of years ago.'

Simon's hand shot up. 'I know. It's Jesus' birthday.'

'That's right, Simon,' said Miss Barnes. 'Do you know the story of Jesus' birth?'

'Yes. Miss Davies, our junior church leader told us.'

'Would you like to tell the rest of the class?'

'I'll try,' said Simon.

'Come along then and sit on my chair and I'll sit in your place on the floor.'

So Simon went to the front of the class. He felt very important sitting on Miss Barnes' chair.

'I'm not sure what comes first,' he said.

'I think you'd better tell us about Jesus' mummy and daddy first,' said Miss Barnes.

'That's Mary and Joseph ... and they were walking along the road one day ...'

'Do you know where they were going?' asked Miss Barnes.

'Bethlehem,' said Simon.

'Was it a long way to Bethlehem?' asked Victoria.

Simon thought for a minute and then said, 'It must have been because Mary had to ride on their donkey.'

'Didn't they have a car?' asked Luke.

'Nobody had a car in those days,' said Miss Barnes, 'so all their things had to be fastened on to the donkey.'

'The donkey would be very tired if Mary was riding on him as well,' said Victoria.

'I'm sure he was – but he was very strong and he probably didn't mind Mary riding on his back. Let Simon tell us what happened when they eventually got to Bethlehem.'

'Joseph knocked on a lot of doors to ask for somewhere to stay but there was no room anywhere.'

'What did they do?' asked Victoria.

'Joseph knocked on the door of an inn,' said Simon. 'And the innkeeper said he didn't have any bedrooms but they could sleep in the stable with the animals.'

'Yuk! I bet that was dirty and smelly,' said Luke turning up his nose.

'I expect it was,' said Miss Barnes. 'But it was better than sleeping on the roadside.'

'How many beds were there?' asked Victoria.

'There weren't any beds,' said Miss Barnes. 'They had to sleep on the floor; on the straw.'

Victoria pulled a face.

'It would be a bit prickly,' she said.

'Yes, I expect so. Now listen carefully while Simon tells us the exciting bit,' said Miss Barnes.

'Mary's baby was born,' he said. 'And they decided to call him Jesus.'

'Where did he sleep, Miss Barnes?' asked Luke.

'In the manger. Do you all know what a manger is?'

'I don't,' said Victoria.

'It's like a basket that holds the animals' food. In those days it may have been made of stone and it probably already had sweet-smelling hay in it so Mary would be able to lay Jesus in it as soon as he was born.'

'She'd need a blanket,' said Victoria.

'She'd taken everything with her because God had told her she was going to have a very special baby. She was going to have God's son. And because he was very special everyone wanted to visit him.'

'Who told them he'd been born?' asked Luke.

'An angel did,' said Simon. 'Some shepherds were in a field looking after their sheep and it was very dark and God sent an angel to tell them that Jesus had been born. So they decided to go and visit him.

'And some wise men saw a bright star in the sky and knew he had been born,' went on Simon, 'so they decided to visit him as well.'

Luke found this story very exciting and wanted to know why they were called wise men.

'Because they knew everything,' said Simon.

'They knew that God had sent Jesus to be king,' Miss Barnes explained. 'So before they visited Jesus they went to Jerusalem to tell King Herod and of course he was very jealous.'

'Why was he jealous, Miss Barnes?' asked Victoria.

'Because the wise men told him that Jesus would be king,' replied Miss Barnes. 'And that meant that King Herod would no longer be king.'

'What did he do?' asked Luke.

'He told the wise men to go and find out where Jesus was and to come back and let him know. He wanted to get rid of Jesus,' said Miss Barnes.

'I bet he wanted to kill him,' whispered Luke.

Victoria looked quite shocked. 'Did they tell him, Miss Barnes? Did they tell him where Jesus was?'

'You must wait and hear the rest of the story.'

Simon went on to tell them how the wise men followed the star which led them to Jesus and how they took him presents of gold, frankincense and myrrh.

'These were very special presents,' said Miss Barnes, 'because they were for a special baby who was going to be king. God's son.'

'Did the wise men go back and tell King Herod where Jesus was?' asked Victoria.

'No,' said Simon. 'They went another way home. God warned them in a dream that King Herod wanted to kill Jesus.'

'That shows that God wanted to protect Jesus doesn't it, Miss Barnes?' said Victoria.

'It certainly does ...' Miss Barnes stood up. 'You told the story of Jesus' birth beautifully, thank you Simon. It's called the Nativity and as part of our school Christmas concert our class is going to act out the Nativity.'

'What will we have to do?' asked Victoria.

'I think you'd better have your break now and we'll talk about it afterwards,' said Miss Barnes.

After the mid-morning break they decided who should act out the parts in the Nativity play. Victoria would be Mary, Simon would be Joseph and Luke would be the innkeeper.

'We also need wise men,' said Miss Barnes. 'Would you like to be one of them, Nigel? And ... let me see ... James and Ralph will you be the other two?'

Ralph's hand shot up.

'We'll need presents to take,' he said. 'What can we use for presents, Miss Barnes?'

'We'll wrap some boxes in gold-coloured paper, shall we? pretend it's gold, frankincense and myrrh.'

'Everybody brought presents when Sally was born,' said Simon.

'I'm sure they did because the birth of a baby is a very special occasion,' said Miss Barnes. 'And then every year afterwards we buy presents on their birthday to show that we love them.

'That's why we buy presents on Christmas day

because it's Jesus' birthday. So I hope on Christmas morning, when you open your presents you'll remember that it's Jesus' birthday that you're celebrating.'

'I will!' said Simon.

'And I will!' said Luke. And all the other children shouted, 'AND I WILL!'

When all the children had been given a part they discussed what they should wear. Some would be shepherds and some angels and they all said their mums would help make the costumes.

'Now, what else will we need?' asked Miss Barnes.

'A donkey,' said Luke.

'I have a donkey,' said Victoria, 'that my Aunty Beth brought me back from Spain. We could use that.'

'That's not big enough,' said Luke. 'Mary wouldn't be able to sit on that. I know someone who's got a real one.'

'I'm not sure that's a good idea, Luke,' said Miss Barnes. 'He may get frightened amongst so many people.'

'Well how is Mary going to ride on a donkey?'

'Perhaps we could begin the Nativity play where she is resting on the road side,' suggested Miss Barnes, 'and Joseph could go off and look for somewhere to stay.'

'What about the baby?' asked Victoria. 'Where are we going to get a baby?'

'We could have your baby sister, couldn't we Simon? Do you think your mum would let us?' said Luke.

'Sally isn't a baby any more, she's seven months old – she wouldn't fit in the manger.'

'We can have my Belinda,' said Victoria, 'because she is my baby.'

'What a good idea,' said Miss Barnes. 'And we can use the model of the stable that we have used other years so that won't be a problem.'

And so when everything was arranged they had to start learning their parts. They practised every day for two weeks until it was time for the Christmas concert. All the parents came to watch and some of the grandparents as well. They all said how good the children were at playing the parts. I'm sure Jesus was pleased too.

Are you pleased when it is Jesus' birthday?

The joys of Christmas

It was still dark when Simon woke on Christmas morning and he could only just see the large, red stocking hanging on the bottom of his bed. It was full of presents and he couldn't wait to open them, so he hopped out of bed, put on his blue dressing-gown, grabbed Little Ted and ran with the stocking into Mummy and Daddy's bedroom.

'He's been, he's been!' he shouted excitedly. 'Mummy, Daddy, wake up! Father Christmas has been.'

'Oh, no,' Daddy groaned. 'What time is it?'

'I don't know but he's been.'

Simon jumped on the bed, sat Little Ted on the pillow and, snuggling in between Mummy and Daddy, started to fumble inside the red stocking. He pulled out a square parcel wrapped in green Christmasy paper.

'It's a jigsaw puzzle and look at this,' he said as he pulled out another present, 'a book about dinosaurs – great!'

Just then they heard Sally, Simon's baby sister, gurgling in her cot.

'I wonder whether Father Christmas has brought

Sally any toys – I'll go and see,' he said jumping out of bed and dashing into Sally's bedroom. 'He has! He has! Mummy come and see!'

Mummy put her head round Sally's bedroom door and Sally chuckled. Then she picked her out of her cot and they all went back into Mummy and Daddy's bed; Simon carrying Sally's Christmas stocking.

By now Daddy was wide awake and so they opened all the presents together. There was coloured wrapping paper and glittery string everywhere.

'Haven't you forgotten something?' said Mummy.

Simon thought for a minute and then gave Mummy, Daddy and Sally a big kiss. 'Happy Christmas, everybody,' he said.

'Happy Christmas, darling,' said Mummy and Daddy.

'Can I go and wish Granny a Happy Christmas now if she's awake?' asked Simon.

'I defy anybody to sleep through the racket you've been making this morning,' said Daddy as he ruffled Simon's hair. 'I bet she wishes she was spending Christmas at home where it's peaceful and quiet.'

'Oh, no I don't,' said Granny, as she came into the bedroom. 'Happy Christmas, everyone.'

'Happy Christmas, Granny,' said Simon as he ran up to her and gave her a big hug. 'Come and look at my presents.'

'I'll go downstairs and make us all a cup of tea,' said Mummy.

As she walked through the hall she noticed something under the Christmas tree.

'Oh, my goodness. What's this?' she said. 'Simon come and see what's down here!'

Simon dashed downstairs and there, set out under the Christmas tree was a train set with an engine and four carriages. He couldn't believe his eyes.

'This is just what I wanted, Mummy, but I didn't think I'd get one. Daddy! Granny! come and see what I've got.'

Daddy, and Granny carrying Sally, came downstairs.

'That's just what *I* wanted,' said Daddy.

Simon knew he was teasing.

'You can have a go after I've had a go, if you like,' he said as he bent down to inspect the green and black engine. 'It's great! I don't know what to play with first.'

'You'll have plenty of time to play with everything when we get back from church,' said Daddy.

'I'll leave Little Ted with my train set. He can be the engine driver 'til I get back if he wants.'

As they walked to church it started to snow.

'Goody, goody!' said Simon. 'We'll be able to make a snowman. Do you think there'll be enough snow by the time we come out of church, Daddy?'

'There might be,' he said.

Simon loved Christmas morning in church. He loved the Nativity scene set out in the children's corner, with the figures of Joseph and Mary looking down at baby Jesus lying in the manger.

And there was a real Christmas tree with its Christmas lights twinkling and lighting up the big oak doorway.

The Vicar told the Christmas story and reminded everyone that they shouldn't forget what they were celebrating.

When they knelt down to say prayers Simon said his own little prayer.

'Happy Birthday, Lord Jesus and thank you for all my presents. I hope you get lots of presents too.'

On the way out he said to Mummy, 'Do you think

that Jesus will get birthday presents, Mummy?'

'We can give him presents. I'm sure one would be for everyone to be friendly towards one another, not just today but every day,' she said.

As they reached the doorway, Simon let go of Daddy's hand and dashed outside.

'Look at the snow,' he said. 'We'll be able to make a snowman won't we, Daddy?'

'It's a long time since I made a snowman,' said a voice behind him. It was Mr Gregory from the corner shop.

'You could come and help Daddy and me make one if you like,' said Simon.

'I expect Mr Gregory has to get home, haven't you?' said Mummy.

'No,' Mr Gregory looked sad. 'As you know I live on my own, so I don't bother to cook a big Christmas dinner just for me. I'm in no rush to get home.'

'In that case you must come and spend Christmas day with us,' said Daddy, with a big smile.

'Oh ...' said Mr Gregory.

'I insist,' said Mummy. 'We would love to have you.'

'Please say yes,' said Simon as he tried to catch the snowflakes, 'then you can help us make a snowman.'

'Well that's very kind of you. I shall have to nip home first and feed little Tibby, my cat. I think I'd better get my Wellington boots too if I'm going to make a snowman.'

'Don't be long!' called Simon, as he ran on ahead sliding in the snow.

When Mr Gregory got back to his shop, Tibby came running to greet him.

'I've been invited to Simon's house, Tibby. Aren't people kind? I shall have to take them a present,' he said as he went through to the shop.

He took a large box of chocolates off the shelf and wrapped it in shiny, gold paper. After he had fed Tibby he put his Wellington boots in the car and drove to Simon's house.

Simon and Daddy were already in the garden when he got there and it was snowing so hard that they looked like snowmen themselves.

'Come and help us,' shouted Simon. 'Mummy and Granny are making the Christmas dinner.'

Mr Gregory put on his Wellington boots and helped to pile up the snow for the snowman's body. Then they rolled a snowball all around the garden until it collected enough snow to make the snowman's head.

'Doesn't he look grand?' said Mr Gregory. 'Let's try and find two pebbles for his eyes.'

'How about two of your marbles, Simon?' said Daddy.

'Yes,' he shouted as he dashed indoors, 'and I'll ask Mummy for a carrot for his nose and a piece of red apple for his mouth.'

They finished off the snowman and then all trudged into the kitchen, cold, wet and hungry – but happy.

'My goodness something smells good,' said Mr Gregory.

'We're having turkey and Christmas pudding,' said Simon. 'Yummy.'

They all sat around the table which looked very Christmasy with its red serviettes and crackers.

'Could I say the prayers today?' Mr Gregory asked. 'I've something special I want to say.'

Everyone bowed their heads while Mr Gregory said, 'Thank you Jesus for this wonderful meal and for the joy of friends at Christmas. Thank you for taking care of me today. Amen.'

And everyone said, 'Amen.'

The Christmas dinner was lovely – and would you believe? Simon was almost too full for Christmas pudding!

After dinner, Mummy took Sally upstairs for her sleep and the grown-ups settled down for a little nap as well. Simon was too excited to sleep so he played with his Christmas toys and especially his train set.

'It's my turn now, Little Ted. You've been the engine driver all morning,' he said.

At five o'clock Mummy said, 'Anybody hungry?'

'Not really,' said Granny.

'I could eat a sandwich,' said Daddy, who was always hungry.

'I should be getting home,' said Mr Gregory. 'My Tibby will be wondering where I've got to.'

Simon dashed over to look out of the window. It was quite dark, but his snowman stood out in the light of the moon and it had stopped snowing.

'Come and look at the snowman, Mr Gregory. His eyes are shining.'

Mr Gregory wandered over to the window. 'That was a good idea to use marbles for eyes,' he said.

Simon rubbed the window with his hand and pressed his nose on the glass.

'Do you think he'll melt? I hope he won't.'

'He will eventually; when it gets warmer. But look at the fun it gave the three of us while we were making him. The snow has been another present from Jesus. And there's something else I'd like to say,' said Mr Gregory. 'Thank you all for a wonderful Christmas day – one of the best I can remember.'

When Mr Gregory had gone home Simon said,

'Mummy, do you think that Jesus would be pleased that we had Mr Gregory to stay with us today?'

'I know he would, darling. It was the best Christmas present we could have given to Jesus.'

Snowman

Snowman bright
in the frosty night.

Please will you stay?

Don't melt away
in the warmth of the day.

The Easter present

Simon was staying at his Granny's house for a few days before Easter.

'What are you doing?' he said as he watched her sewing little pieces of material together.

'I'm making a patchwork quilt for your bed,' said Granny.

Simon rummaged through the bag of material. 'Here's a piece of fur,' he said, digging deeper into the bag. 'Is it a piece of Napoleon's fur?'

'It is. I keep promising Napoleon I'll make him some new ears but I haven't got round to it yet.'

'They are a bit scraggy, aren't they, Granny?'

'Well, he is very old. He was Daddy's teddy bear and he still sits up there in Daddy's bedroom where you sleep when you come to stay with me.'

'I know, and sometimes I sit Little Ted next to Napoleon on the floor so that he won't be lonely.'

Simon looked inside the bag of material and pulled out another piece of material. It was red and white striped.

'What did you make out of this Granny?' he asked.

She took a closer look. 'That's a piece of Daddy's

beach shorts. He used to love going to the beach with his bucket and spade. "I'm going to dig for treasure", he used to say.'

'Can we go to the beach tomorrow?'

'If it's a nice day. I'll make a picnic.'

'And I'll take my bucket and spade out of the shed,' Simon said excitedly, 'then I can dig for treasure. I don't think I'll take Little Ted with me, I'll leave him with Napoleon for company.'

The next day was bright and sunny but when they got to the beach it was quite breezy, so Granny sat in the sandhills and Simon dug with his spade.

'There's something hard down here, Granny,' he said. 'Do you think it's treasure?'

Granny went over to have a look. 'I can't tell until you get it out of the sand.'

'It's not very big,' said Simon as he pulled out a little china, sailor doll. 'Who do you think it belongs to?'

'Nobody now. It looks as though it's been buried for years. See how the sea and the sand have washed all his paint away.'

'He's not very handsome, is he? I think I'll throw him away.'

'Perhaps that's how he comes to be buried there, because someone threw him away,' said Granny.

Simon began to feel sorry for the little sailor doll that nobody wanted. 'He can't help it if he's not very handsome, can he? Can we take him down to the sea and give him a wash?'

When Simon had swished the doll around in the water a bit, Granny said, 'My goodness, that's an improvement. Even though all his paint is chipped he still has his lovely smile.'

'Do you think someone used to love him like I love Little Ted?'

'I'm sure they did,' she said.

'I couldn't ever throw Little Ted away.'

'And Daddy didn't throw Napoleon away even though he's got scraggy ears,' said Granny.

Simon thought about this. 'I wonder whether someone will come back to look for him?'

'I shouldn't think so – not now.'

'Can I take him home with me?'

'If you're going to take care of him then I think it'll be all right.'

So Simon put the little sailor doll in his bucket and took it back to Granny's house.

When they arrived he took it straight up to his bedroom.

'Look what I found, Little Ted,' he said. 'I found it when I was digging for treasure. He's not very handsome but he's got a lovely smile hasn't he?'

The following day Daddy came to collect Simon. 'Have you had a good time?' he said.

'Yes. We went to the beach and guess what I dug up?'

Simon dashed up to his bedroom to get the little sailor doll.

'Treasure!' shouted Daddy.

'No,' Simon said as he came running down the stairs. 'This sailor doll. He's not very handsome but he has a lovely smile.'

Daddy looked at it closely. 'He only needs a touch of paint,' he said. 'That wouldn't be much of a job. He hasn't lost all his paint so we should be able to see the colours we'll need.'

At home the next morning Simon took out his box of

paints and sat with Daddy at the kitchen table to paint the little doll.

'It looks as though his shirt was red and white striped,' said Daddy. So he painted that first.

'Can I paint something?' asked Simon excitedly.

'You can paint his trousers. They're green.'

Simon dipped his paintbrush in the green paint and very carefully painted the sailor doll's trousers.

'That's very good but we'd better leave it to dry before we do any more,' said Daddy, 'or all the colours will run together.'

Later on Daddy painted the sailor doll's yellow necktie and then he painted his blue sash. Simon painted his brown boots and blue cap.

'What's he got in his hand?' Simon asked.

Daddy looked closely. 'I think it's a cutlass – a sword used by sailors.'

'He doesn't look very fierce, does he?' said Simon.

'Not with a lovely, big smile like that,' laughed Daddy.

'Well we'll need to paint it, and we haven't painted his face yet. Shall we do that now, Daddy?'

'Let's leave it until the rest of him is dry. We'll do it after tea.'

By the time Simon went to bed the little sailor doll was completely dry.

'My goodness,' said Mummy. 'Isn't he handsome? I wouldn't have recognised him. What are you going to do with him?'

'I haven't decided yet,' said Simon.

Simon stood him on the chest of drawers in his bedroom next to Little Ted. The little sailor doll smiled at Simon and Simon smiled back.

'D'you know, Little Ted, when you smile at someone

they smile back at you and that makes both of you feel better?'

At breakfast Simon said, 'I've been thinking about what to do with my little sailor doll.'

'Oh, yes,' said Daddy as he buttered another piece of toast. 'And what have you decided?'

'I might give him to Granny. It could be her Easter present from me.'

'What a lovely idea,' said Mummy.

'But ...' said Simon.

'What's the matter? You don't sound very sure.'

'Well, I love him very much now that he's painted and he cheers me up when he smiles at me.'

'It's very difficult to part with something that you love, isn't it, darling?' said Mummy.

'Sometimes we have to do things that are difficult,' said Daddy. 'Remember it's Easter time – the time that God gave his only son, Jesus, to die on the cross for our sins. That must have been very difficult for him.'

'I know,' said Simon. 'But I've *already* got Little Ted to love, haven't I?'

'Yes. And Mummy, Daddy, baby sister Sally and Granny as well,' said Mummy.

So Simon decided to give Granny the little sailor doll when she came for tea on Easter Sunday. Mummy gave him a box to put him in and as he was wrapping it he said, 'Mummy did you know that I was really looking for treasure when I found the little sailor doll, but I didn't find any?'

'I think you did,' said Mummy. 'Because treasure is anything that is very precious and the sailor doll is very precious isn't he?'

'He is to me because I made him new again, didn't I?' said Simon.

'You did. And you've decided to give him to Granny because you love her, just as God gave us Jesus because he loved us. It must have been hard for him to give up something so precious.'

Simon thought about this. 'Will Granny think my sailor doll is very precious?' he asked.

'I'm sure she will,' said Mummy.

When Granny arrived on Easter Sunday, Simon gave her the present. She opened the box carefully and the little sailor doll smiled up at her and Granny smiled back.

'He's lovely, darling,' she said as she gave Simon a big hug. 'I can't believe how handsome he looks now that he's painted. Are you sure you can bear to part with him?'

'Yes, 'cos I've got Little Ted and you haven't got anyone. I know you've got Napoleon but he really belongs to Daddy so I want you to have someone of your very own to love.'

'Thank you very much,' she said. 'I'll treasure him always. And every morning when I wake up he'll smile at me and I'll smile back and then we'll both be happy.'

The patchwork quilt

Granny's sewing coloured squares
to make a patchwork quilt
some are smooth like shiny glass
some as soft as silk.

There's bits with spots and squares and dots
and some with wiggly stripes
she lets me rummage in her bag
to choose the bits I like.

She sews and sews
and then it
grows
and
grows
and
grows
and
grows.
And when it's finished Granny said
it'll make a cover for my bed.

Napoleon bear

Napoleon bear
is furry and fat
he's round as a dumpling
and sits on the mat.

His legs are short
so he's not very tall
because he's unsteady
he leans on the wall.

Simon's hospital visit

'Mummy, Mummy!' screamed Simon. 'Mummy, help me, Mummy!'

Mummy dashed out of the house and there was Simon lying on the ground with his bicycle on top of him.

'Oh, darling. What did you do?' she asked as she lifted the bicycle off him.

'I toppled over and bumped my head and hurt my knee,' he cried.

Mummy took off his helmet and held him in her arms. 'There, there,' she said, patting his back to comfort him. But still he kept on crying.

'I've lost my glasses,' he said. 'My new ones like Daddy's.'

'No, you haven't,' said Mummy. 'Here they are. They've landed on the lawn so they're not broken. Show me where it hurts,' she said as she brushed his hair out of his eyes.

'Here and here,' he said pointing to his head and his knee.

Mummy inspected his leg and asked him to wiggle his toes.

'It seems to be all right,' she said.

'But it hurts a lot,' Simon sniffed.

'Can you stand on it? Let me help you,' Mummy said as she lifted him gently.

'It's very sore,' he said, 'and my head aches.'

'I think I'd better take you along to the hospital and let them have a look at you,' Mummy said as she carried him into the kitchen and sat him on a chair.

'No! no! I don't want to go to the hospital,' he cried.

'It's all right,' Mummy tried to calm him. 'The doctor will just check you over – he won't hurt you. I'll ask Jeremy's mummy to keep an eye on Sally – she's asleep in her pram at the moment.'

So Mummy pushed Simon's baby sister into the garden next door and then took Simon to the hospital.

Simon was very frightened when they went through the big glass doors into the reception area. He hopped on one leg from the car and sat on a chair while Mummy told the doctor what had happened.

'Let's have a look at you, young man,' said the doctor and he lifted Simon on to a long couch and drew the curtains around him.

'I remember falling off my bike when I was a little boy like you,' he said as he looked at Simon's leg.

'Did you cry?' Simon asked.

'I seem to remember I did. I think it was because I was frightened of what they might do to me at the hospital.'

'I'm frightened,' said Simon.

'Well there's no need to be. I'm not going to hurt you.

'First of all I'm going to ask the nurse to take you to the X-Ray Department. We'll get a photograph of your leg and your head, just to make sure you haven't damaged anything.'

But Simon didn't want his picture taken.

'It's all right,' said the doctor, 'it's just like having your photograph taken when you're on holiday. But the picture shows us what you look like inside instead of outside.'

The nurse pushed Simon to the X-Ray Department in a wheelchair. Mummy went with him. A lady in a white coat was there to take the X-rays but the camera was much bigger than the one Simon's father used.

'I want you to take a big breath and keep very still,' said the lady, 'because if you move the pictures will be blurred.'

Simon didn't feel a thing; it was just like when Daddy took his photograph.

'You were very good,' said the lady in the white coat. 'I'm sure we'll have some good pictures of your leg and your head.'

When the X-rays had been developed the doctor put them in a frame in front of a light to look at them.

'Is that the inside of my head?' asked Simon.

'It is,' said the doctor. 'This, here, is your bony skull that protects your brain.'

'I wear a helmet to protect my brain,' said Simon.

'It's a good job otherwise you might have done some serious damage.' The doctor looked carefully at the X-ray. 'Everything seems to be all right,' he said.

'Can you see what I'm thinking?' asked Simon.

The doctor smiled. 'I wish we could. We'd really be clever if we could do that.'

'God knows what we're thinking, so he's clever, isn't he?'

'He certainly is,' said the doctor. 'And he knows without looking at an X-ray.'

'What's the other X-ray?' asked Simon.

'It's a picture of the bone inside your leg. It isn't broken; in fact everything seems to be fine but I think we'll keep you in overnight. Your headache should have gone by then.'

But Simon wanted to go home.

'Mummy can stay with you if she wishes,' said the doctor.

'But I haven't got my pyjamas and my toothbrush and my Little Ted,' said Simon.

'I'll go and get them, darling, and I'll tell Daddy where we are. He should be home from work very soon,' said Mummy.

The nurse took Simon up to the children's ward and put him in a little room with four other children. There were lovely Walt Disney pictures on the wall and in the middle of the room was a table piled high with toys. There was also a television set standing in the corner.

The nurse sat Simon on a chair near the table and he helped one of the other boys build a castle.

When Mummy returned, Daddy and Sally came with her.

'I don't want to stay here all night, Daddy,' Simon said.

'It's only for tonight. And Mummy is staying with you.'

'You're very lucky,' Mummy said. 'Some of the children have to stay in much longer than you – especially the ones who are very poorly.'

Simon thought about this and then said, 'Will they get better?'

'If God thinks that's best for them,' said Mummy. 'He will help the doctors and nurses to make them better.'

The next morning Simon was awake early. The nurses

were busy in the ward. Some were washing the patients, and some were making beds.

'Can I go home now?' he asked the nurse who came to make his bed.

'Not just yet,' she said. 'You need to see the doctor first. He'll be here later.'

After he'd had his wash, a nurse came to take his temperature. She asked him to hold the thermometer underneath his arm and to keep very still so that he wouldn't break it.

'Why are you taking my temperature?' he asked.

'To see how hot you are,' she said.

After a minute she took the little glass thermometer from under his arm and looked carefully at it.

'Am I very hot?' Simon asked.

'You're just right,' she said.

When the doctor arrived Simon said, 'Can I go home now please?'

'We'll see. You'd better climb out of bed first and let me see you walk.'

So Simon took a few steps hanging on to his bed.

'Mm. You won't be riding your bike for a while but your leg should improve in a day or two. How does your head feel?' asked the doctor.

'My headache's gone now and my temperature's just right,' said Simon.

'Is it now? OK, I think you're well enough to go home this morning – but remember no riding your bike until your leg is better.'

So Mummy collected all Simon's things together and the nurse came to say goodbye, but just as Simon got out of bed Little Ted toppled on to the floor.

'Oh, Little Ted,' he said. 'Have you hurt yourself?'

'Is he all right?' asked the nurse.

'He's bumped his head,' said Simon.

'Let me see. Perhaps I'd better put a bandage on it just to be on the safe side,' she said.

When Simon got home, Jeremy his best friend from next door, came round to see him.

'Are you better?' he asked.

'Yes, thank you,' said Simon. 'The nurses and doctor and the X-ray lady made me better. It was God who showed them what to do because he's very clever.'

'What's an X-ray lady?' asked Jeremy.

'She's a lady in a white coat who takes the photographs of the inside of your body.'

'The inside of your body!' said Jeremy in alarm. 'Does it hurt?'

'No, it's just like having your photograph taken at home,' said Simon. 'And then the doctor lets you see them.'

'I don't think I'd like to go to hospital,' said Jeremy.

'It's all right, really. And there's lots of toys to play with on the ward.'

'Why has Little Ted got that bandage on his head?' asked Jeremy.

'He bumped his head. Didn't you Little Ted?' said Simon as he gave his favourite bear a big hug.

'He looks like Pudsey Bear,' said Jeremy.

'The nurse put the bandage on but it's slipped down. Here let me fix it,' said Simon as he pushed it up so that Little Ted could see out of his eye.

'Did *he* have to have an X-ray?' asked Jeremy.

'No. It wasn't bad enough for an X-ray. It wasn't as bad as the bump I had on my head because he only fell out of bed; he didn't fall off his bike like me,' Simon said as he laid Little Ted down on the settee to rest.

Simon's summer holiday

'I'm glad your mummy let you come on holiday with us,' said Simon to Jeremy as Daddy drove the car into the caravan park.

'So am I,' said Jeremy. 'I've never stayed in a caravan before.'

As soon as Mummy had unlocked the caravan door Simon and Jeremy dashed inside and Sally, Simon's baby sister, toddled after them. Simon lifted her up the step because she was only one year old.

'This is where we sleep,' said Simon.

'Oh, goody, they're bunk-beds. Can I sleep in the top one?' asked Jeremy, climbing up to have a look.

'If you like. I usually sleep up there but because you're my best friend I'll let you,' said Simon as he dashed about opening doors.

'Sally sleeps in this room here with Mummy and Daddy and this is a little shower room. We have a cooker as well and you can come to the shop with me every morning for the bread and milk 'cos I know where it is.'

Simon and Jeremy emptied their bags. They put their shorts and T-shirts in the drawer under the bottom bunk-bed and their coats in the tall, narrow wardrobe.

'Can we go out now, Mummy?' asked Simon.

'Where are you going? I don't want you wandering too far, tea will be ready in half an hour.'

'I'll just show Jeremy around the caravan park,' he said as he jumped down the step. 'Come on Jeremy, follow me!'

They went all around the caravan park. Simon showed Jeremy where the shop was and pointed out the path that led to the hill behind. As they were walking back to their caravan they met Jonathan, who was seven and his brother Matthew, who was twelve. Simon knew them very well because they came for their holidays every year.

'Hi Simon!' said Matthew. 'Where are you going?'

'Just going back for tea,' said Simon.

'We've been to the beach,' Jonathan said, scraping his spade along the path.

'Ooh, where's the beach?' asked Jeremy.

'Down that path there, just behind those trees,' explained Simon.

'Jeremy's my best friend,' he said to Matthew and Jonathan. 'He hasn't stayed in a caravan before.'

'You'll like it here,' said Matthew. 'There's lots to do. What are you doing tomorrow?' he asked Simon. 'We're going to the beach again, want to come?'

'I'll ask Mummy and Daddy,' said Simon.

When they got back to the caravan Simon asked Mummy whether they could go to the beach tomorrow with Matthew and Jonathan.

'We'll see,' she said. 'We've not decided anything yet.'

After Simon and Jeremy had finished their supper

they said their prayers and hopped into bed.

Jeremy couldn't get to sleep and he started to cry.

'What's the matter?' Simon whispered.

'I'm missing Mummy.'

'You'll be all right,' said Simon. 'My mummy's here.'

'But it's not the same, she doesn't belong to me.'

'Haven't you got anything with you that belongs?'

'No,' said Jeremy, and started to cry even louder.
'I take my Little Ted with me everywhere then I can
talk to him when I'm lonely.'

Mummy heard Jeremy crying and opened the bedroom door. 'What's the matter?' she whispered.

'I want my mummy,' he cried, 'and I haven't got anything that belongs.'

Simon thought for a few minutes and then said,
'Would you like to borrow my Little Ted just for
tonight?'

'But then you won't have anything that belongs,'
sniffed Jeremy.

'But I've got my mummy if I need her,' said Simon
as he passed Little Ted to Jeremy.

'And I'll be your mummy too while we're on holiday
if you like, Jeremy,' said Simon's mummy. So Jeremy
held out his arms and Simon's mummy gave him a big
hug. Then he cuddled up to Little Ted and very
quickly went to sleep.

The next morning Matthew and Jonathan came to call
for Simon and Jeremy.

'We're going into town to do some shopping,' said
Mummy.

'Oh, do we have to go with you?' said Simon,
looking miserable. 'Can't we go with Matthew and
Jonathan to the beach?'

'How long will you be, Matthew?' Daddy asked.

'I've promised Mum we'll be back by twelve,' said Matthew.

'Right,' said Daddy. 'But no going in the sea. It's too choppy today.'

'We're only going on the beach,' said Jonathan.

'I'll look after them all,' said Matthew who was a very sensible boy for his age.

'Thank you, thank you,' shouted Simon excitedly as he jumped up to kiss Daddy goodbye.

'And don't forget, back at twelve,' said Mummy.

'We will. I promise,' Simon said as he jumped down the caravan steps.

'I've got my watch on, Mrs Hurst,' said Matthew, 'so I'll keep an eye on the time.'

When they arrived on the beach it was cold and windy so they played cricket for a little while to get warm. Then Matthew said, 'I've got some orange squash in my rucksack. Let's find some shelter while we drink it.'

So they clambered over a little wall and into the sandhills where the spiky grass prickled their legs. Behind the sandhills was a barbed wire fence surrounding a field of sheep.

As they were drinking their squash Jonathan said, 'Hush! I can hear something.'

'What is it?' whispered Simon.

'It's a sort of whimpering. Let's go and look.'

Lying on the path was a black and white puppy – his nose covered in sand. When he saw the boys he tried to get to his feet but then flopped down again.

'Look at his paw!' gasped Jeremy. 'It's bleeding.'

'He's gashed it on this barbed wire,' said Matthew as he bent down to inspect it.

Simon stroked the puppy's head and gazed across the field. 'He must live at that farm over there. Shall we take him home?'

'I'll carry him. You bring my rucksack,' said Matthew.

As they walked up to the farmhouse, a black and white sheep dog ran to greet them. She jumped up at Matthew.

'Get down, Molly,' said the farmer. 'She's excited to see you. That's her pup ... I wondered where he'd got to ... Haven't seen him all morning.'

'He's cut his paw on the barbed wire,' said Jonathan.

'Oh, dear. Let me have a look ... Mm, I don't think it's too deep.' Molly jumped up at the puppy again and the farmer tried to drag her away.

'You'd best put him down,' he said, 'before she knocks you over.'

Matthew put the little dog on the floor and Molly nuzzled him affectionately. Then she saw his injured foot and started to lick it.

'She'll probably lick it better,' said the farmer. 'It was very good of you to bring him home – Molly doesn't usually let him out of her sight. He must have slipped away while she was rounding up the sheep this morning. Would you like to come into the farmhouse for a drink?'

Matthew looked at his watch. 'Er, no thank you. It's twelve o'clock–we ought to be getting back.'

'Staying at the caravan park, are you?' asked the farmer.

Matthew nodded his head.

'Well any time you want to come and see Danny ... that's the pup's name, you'll be very welcome. I think Molly would like to see you again too.'

Molly jumped up and Matthew patted her on the head. Then she flopped down and started to lick Danny's cut paw.

'She'll soon have it right,' said the farmer.

By the time they had crossed the field back on to the beach and then walked to the caravan park it was nearly one o'clock. Simon's Mummy and Daddy were frantic with worry.

'Where on earth have you been?' shouted Daddy. He was obviously very cross and his loud voice made Sally cry.

'I'm really sorry, Mr Hurst. It's my fault,' explained Matthew.

'It's no use being sorry,' said Daddy. 'You promised to bring Simon and Jeremy home for twelve o'clock. We've been worried out of our minds.'

Simon felt uncomfortable. Daddy didn't usually get so cross and raise his voice – especially to one of Simon's friends.

'I can explain, Daddy,' said Simon.

'I'm not interested in explanations. Matthew broke his promise.'

'Let Simon explain, dear,' said Mummy.

So Simon told how they had found the injured puppy and taken him back to the farmhouse. And how the farmer had been grateful and Molly had been pleased to get Danny back.

'You see,' said Mummy. 'I said there would be a good reason for them being late. Matthew doesn't usually break his promise.'

'But the reason might have been that they had been swept out to sea or one of them had been injured.'

'Well it wasn't, so let's have some lunch. Would you and Jonathan like to join us?' Mummy asked Matthew.

'No thank you, Mrs Hurst – Mum is expecting us. And I'm really sorry we were late.'

Mummy made lunch but none of them felt much

like eating. Everyone was upset; Simon and Jeremy because they had broken a promise and Mummy and Daddy because they had been so worried.

Daddy went out on his own after lunch and, because it was raining, Simon and Jeremy stayed indoors and played Snakes and Ladders.

When Daddy got back Simon said, 'Where've you been, Daddy?'

'I went to apologise to Matthew for the way I spoke to him,' he said. 'I was so upset because you were late that I didn't give any of you a proper chance to explain.'

'Well we're sorry too for being late, aren't we Jeremy?' said Simon.

Jeremy nodded his head.

'Sometimes,' Daddy said, 'when people are very upset they say things they are sorry for afterwards – and Mummy and I were very upset. Do you forgive me for being so cross?'

Simon nodded his head and ran over to give Daddy a big hug.

'Do you forgive me and Jeremy for being late?' said Simon.

'Yes,' said Daddy. 'Whatever you do we will always forgive you.'

'Just like Jesus does even when we do things that don't please him,' said Simon.

'Yes. But we do need to try to put things right, if we can and to learn from our mistakes.'

'Like saying we're sorry,' said Simon.

'Like saying we're sorry,' said Daddy as he gave Simon and Jeremy a big hug.

Other stories suitable for reading aloud to under 6s:

Oliver and the Big Green Snake
Jan Godfrey

'Is that you, Oliver?' called Mum.

Oliver didn't answer. He was looking for a very good hidey-hole for his snowman.

'Come on, snowman,' said Oliver. 'You're going to hide in the food cupboard. You can eat a biscuit if you like.'

A lively and humorous collection of short stories about Oliver, who is almost five. Oliver likes talking to things especially his teddy bear Bruin, but his talks with these imaginary friends often get him into trouble. His real friends Polly and Vimal and Honey the dog also feature in the stories.

Zac and the Multi-coloured Spidajig
Kathleen Crawford

'Yummy!' thought Sophie, 'they look delicious.'

She was just opening her mouth and putting out her tongue to eat the first strawberry when it happened.

'HIC,' went Sophie, and she shot high into the air, completely missing the strawberry she wanted to eat.

Meet Sophie, the frog with hiccups, Zac and his

monster spider called Spidajig and Mrs McMuddle, who goes to buy a loaf of tomato soup.

A book of lively short stories, poems and simple prayers.

Both of these titles are also available as story cassettes.